in the news™

NUKES

THE SPREAD OF NUCLEAR WEAPONS

Steve Minneus

ROSEN
PUBLISHING®

New York

Published in 2 , Inc.
29 East 21st S

Copyright © 2008 by The Rosen Publishing Group, Inc.

First Edition

Library of Congress Cataloging-in-Publication Data

Minneus, Steve.
Nukes: the spread of nuclear weapons / Steve Minneus. — 1st ed.
    p. cm. — (In the news)
Includes bibliographical references and index.
ISBN-13: 978-1-4042-1916-8
ISBN-10: 1-4042-1916-1
1. Nuclear nonproliferation — Juvenile literature. I. Title.
JZ5675.M56 2008
327.1'747 — dc22

                                                           2007001030

Manufactured in the United States of America

On the cover: (Clockwise from bottom right) Mushroom cloud following a June 24, 1957, hydrogen bomb test; a short-range ballistic missile on display during a January 2003 Indian military parade; North Korean People's Army soldiers march in Pyongyang in 2006.

contents

Origins of the Bomb

For more than sixty years, nuclear weapons have cast a frightening shadow over world politics. From their first use in 1945 to the present day, these incredibly destructive weapons have influenced nearly every government's military policy. Today, eight nations have acknowledged that they have nuclear weapons: China, France, India, North Korea, Pakistan, Russia, the United Kingdom, and the United States. Another nation, Israel, is strongly believed to have nuclear weapons, although it has not confirmed this.

Building a nuclear weapon is extremely difficult. It requires teams of scientists, lots of specialized equipment, and systems to contain all of the hazardous waste generated by nuclear processes. While it is possible for most nations with nuclear power plants also to make materials for nuclear weapons, every nation's nuclear activities are closely monitored. Organizations such as the United Nations' International Atomic Energy Agency and treaties such as the Partial Test Ban Treaty and the Nuclear

Non-Proliferation Treaty (NPT) set strict international laws regarding the possession and development of nuclear weapons. But even these safeguards cannot stop nuclear proliferation—the spread of nuclear weapons throughout the world.

The more countries that acquire nuclear weapons, the greater the likelihood that they will eventually be used. In order to persuade nations not to pursue these weapons, international treaties offer rewards to nations that agree to pursue only peaceful nuclear power. Until the day when all nuclear weapons are dismantled, it is possible for new nations to acquire them.

Countries that violate international law often face repercussions from the international community. Virtually every nation in the world is dependent upon other countries for one reason or another. A nation that goes against international law can find itself isolated from the international community, meaning that other countries may not trade with it, offer it aid, or import its goods. This happened in 2006, when a Communist nation decided to test a nuclear weapon.

Recent Developments

World leaders became skeptical of North Korea's nuclear capabilities in 2003, after it withdrew from the NPT, which it had signed in 1985. On October 9, 2006, North Korea

Two women in Tokyo, Japan, read newspaper accounts of North Korea's successful October 9, 2006, underground nuclear test.

detonated a bomb, confirming fears and surprising leaders the world over. By then, it was known that the Communist nation had nuclear weapons, but North Korean leaders gave little warning of the test, alerting China only twenty minutes before setting off the device. At the time of this writing, North Korea is the most recent nation to build and test a nuclear weapon.

North Korea insists that its nuclear weapons are a necessary part of its defense strategy and that the country is fully within its rights to create such weapons. Other nations disagree. Many countries have instituted sanctions against North Korea, meaning that they refuse to trade with, or otherwise provide goods to, the country. Not being able to receive foreign food and medication is a serious blow to the nation, which has been dependent on aid for some time.

Modern-Day Nuclear Threats

Shortly after the United States used the first nuclear bombs in 1945 in World War II, other nations such as the Union of Soviet Socialist Republics (USSR) built up massive stockpiles of thousands of nuclear bombs and missiles during the Cold War (1947–circa 1991). Tense diplomatic relations existed between the United States and the USSR for decades. Luckily, no weapons were used during this conflict. A full-scale nuclear war between the two would have caused unbelievable destruction. The USSR has broken into smaller, independent nations, and many countries have worked to decrease their nuclear stockpiles or get rid of them altogether.

   Changing times have eliminated some nuclear threats and created others. Today, the rise of terrorist activity around the world has been a cause for concern: what would happen if terrorists came into possession of a nuclear weapon? There is also the possibility that terrorists could construct variants of nuclear weapons, called dirty bombs, which do not cause a nuclear reaction but spread radioactive waste.

Who gets to decide which countries get nuclear weapons, and what are the issues involved? Why are certain countries allowed to have weapons while others aren't? If nuclear weapons can create such a diplomatic stir, why are they even allowed at all? To answer these questions, we need to go back more than sixty years to just before World War II, back to the dawn of the nuclear age, when armed conflict changed the face of the world.

Secret Science

In 1939, three physicists—Leo Szilard (1898–1964), Edward Teller (1908–2003), and Eugene Wigner (1902–1995)—made a decision that would ultimately change warfare forever. A process known as nuclear fission had been discovered. In nuclear fission, energy is created by splitting atoms of uranium-235, uranium-233, or plutonium-239. These rare forms of the metallic elements uranium and plutonium are the only things on Earth that can cause a nuclear reaction. It is possible—although difficult—for scientists to "enrich" uranium by separating the molecules of uranium-235 and uranium-233 from normal uranium.

Szilard theorized that a chain reaction of atoms splitting apart could result in a tremendous release of energy. If harnessed, this energy could be used as a source of power—or as a weapon. Fearing the potential misuse of this information, Szilard initially kept his findings to himself. But when other physicists began making similar discoveries, he decided it was time to come forward. If Adolf Hitler (1889–1945) and his Nazi regime, who were by then engaged in a scheme to conquer the world, figured out how to make a weapon with this technology, they could potentially win the war that they had just launched in Europe. That could not be allowed to happen.

Edward Teller is known as the "father of the hydrogen bomb." He also helped develop the atomic bomb during the Manhattan Project of 1942–1945.

The Manhattan Project

A top-secret scientific research laboratory compound was established outside of the desert town of Los Alamos, New Mexico. Los Alamos Laboratory contained some of the brightest minds in engineering and physics. Heading the scientific team was brilliant physicist Robert Oppenheimer (1904–1967). Similar labs were set up elsewhere in the United States, the United Kingdom, and

Canada, under the blanket name the Manhattan Project. Simply put, the goal of the Manhattan Project was to create a nuclear weapon.

Beginning in 1942, the Manhattan Project scientists worked long and hard to create this weapon before the Nazis could. They finally achieved their goal in 1945. The world's first nuclear weapon was tested in the New Mexico desert on July 16 of that year. The test produced something that the world had never seen before: a nuclear explosion. The assembled scientists, technicians, and military personnel were awed as they witnessed the blinding flash.

Fighting the Axis Powers

Nazi Germany joined forces with Japan, Italy, and a number of other countries, forming an alliance known as the Axis powers. The United Kingdom, the USSR, and other countries who opposed the Axis powers became known as the Allied powers, or the Allies. Millions of soldiers and civilians lost their lives in the bitter battles between these two sides. Once-magnificent cities were bombed to rubble as armies rampaged across western Europe, Asia, and beyond.

The United States was drawn into the war on December 7, 1941, when Japanese fighter planes attacked a fleet of American ships in the Pacific near

Pearl Harbor in Hawaii. Hundreds of U.S. servicemen were killed, and the American public was outraged. It didn't take long for U.S. President Franklin D. Roosevelt (1882–1945) to order troops into battle. Americans immediately rallied behind the war effort. Everyone from everyday citizens to professional athletes and movie stars were drafted to fight overseas.

The entry of the United States into the war gave the Allies a much-needed boost, but they weren't out of hot water yet. Tens of millions had already died, and the end of the war was nowhere in sight.

Peace at a Cost

Harry S. Truman (1884–1972) started his presidency of the United States in 1945, and he was determined to bring a swift end to the war. With the assistance of other Allies, he drafted a document known as the Potsdam Declaration. Delivered to the Japanese on July 26, 1945, the Potsdam Declaration offered an ultimatum to the Japanese army—it could either surrender immediately or be destroyed. In the absence of a response from the Japanese, Truman made the decision to drop a nuclear bomb on the Japanese city of Hiroshima.

On August 6, 1945, the first nuclear weapon ever to be used in combat detonated in Hiroshima, Japan. Tens of thousands died in the initial explosion, which

A lone building stands in the ruins of Hiroshima following the dropping of an atomic bomb on the city by American forces in 1945.

destroyed many of the city's buildings. Thousands more would die from radiation and injuries in the days to come. On August 9, 1945, a second bomb was dropped on the city of Nagasaki, Japan. More than 200,000 Japanese citizens died in the bombings.

Japan announced its surrender to the Allies on August 15. The deaths and massive illnesses that these two bombs caused showed the world the devastation that nuclear weapons could cause. It also forced the global community to form one of the main international monitors of nuclear weapons, the United Nations. With the war in Europe effectively over, Japan's surrender signaled the end of World War II. The cost of peace had been incalculably high, unleashing a terrible new weapon on the world.

The Road to Treaties

By the end of the war, large sections of Europe were devastated. As Europe rebuilt, two new world superpowers emerged: the United States and the Soviet Union. Even as the two fought as allies during the war, tension began to build between them. The United States was a democratic nation with a free-market economy, and the Soviet Union was a Communist nation with a state-run economy.

Conflicting global interests resulted in friction between the nations. Each superpower felt that the other was trying to spread its ideology throughout the world. By 1948, the Cold War was in full swing.

The Cold War got its name from the fact that the United States and the Soviet Union never directly engaged in combat with each other. However, both sides began amassing large stockpiles of weapons, including nuclear weapons, in case armed conflict should arise. They also began to develop intercontinental ballistic missiles (ICBMs). These missiles had the ability to

A 1949 political cartoon illustrates the arms race between the United States and Soviet Union following World War II.

deliver a nuclear warhead to a target thousands of miles away.

Nuclear Nations

After World War II, the victorious Allied nations founded the United Nations (UN). This important international organization is dedicated to mediating conflict between nations. The United Nations Security Council is in charge of attempting to maintain a state of peace around the world. There are fifteen "seats" on the UN Security Council. Ten of these seats are temporary, and five are permanent. The five nations that permanently hold seats are the United States, the United Kingdom, Russia, China, and France.

The International Atomic Energy Agency (IAEA) was established by the UN in 1957 and exists to this day. In fact, the agency, headed by Director General Mohamed ElBaradei (1942–), was awarded the Nobel Peace Prize in 2005. The IAEA is devoted to finding peaceful, civilian uses for atomic energy and monitors the proliferation of nuclear weapons and materials around the globe.

However, even international oversight was not enough to curb the buildup of nuclear weapons during the Cold War. Before long, the United States and Soviet Union had numerous nuclear missiles ready to be launched at the slightest provocation. If one country were to attack the other directly, it could result in a nuclear counterattack. A full-on nuclear war between the two nations could have resulted in their total destruction. Some feared it would lead to the destruction of all life on Earth. This situation, which came to be known as "mutually assured destruction," made for tense and paranoid relations between these nations.

A Need for Non-Proliferation

This tension came to a head in 1962, during an event known as the Cuban Missile Crisis. The Soviet Union was attempting to install nuclear weapons in Communist Cuba. Because of Cuba's proximity to the United

The director general of the International Atomic Energy Agency prepares for a meeting.

States, Soviet nuclear ballistic missiles could reach U.S. targets within a matter of minutes.

Conflict was ultimately averted, but the world had come to the brink of nuclear war. The bombing of Hiroshima and Nagasaki had proved that nuclear weapons not only had the potential to kill thousands of people and destroy cities, but also to cause cancer and other deadly health effects in people exposed to radiation. The effects of nuclear explosions could linger long after the initial blast, potentially poisoning the environment for years to come. What would happen if hundreds of nuclear weapons were used, ones much more powerful than those dropped on Japan in 1945? What if thousands were used? The magnitude of such destruction would be unimaginable.

Treaties

After the Cuban Missile Crisis had ended, the United States and the Soviet Union began taking steps to curb their expanding nuclear arsenals. Each already had enough nuclear weapons to destroy the other's major cities many times over. The world recognized that this powerful new technology needed to be regulated.

Partial Test Ban Treaty

In 1963, the Partial Test Ban Treaty was put into effect. Overseen by the IAEA, the treaty was the first of many

U.S. president John F. Kennedy *(seated)* signs the Partial Test Ban Treaty in 1963 as U.S. senators and Vice President Lyndon Johnson *(far right)* look on.

international agreements to control and monitor the spread of nuclear weapons. Currently ratified by more than 100 countries, the Partial Test Ban Treaty prohibits countries from testing nuclear weapons in the air, water, and even outer space, although it makes no provision against underground testing. The Partial Test Ban Treaty was one of the first steps taken to stop the spread of nuclear weapons. Since then, there have been a number of other treaties that have sought to limit the spread and misuse of nuclear weapons.

Nuclear Non-Proliferation Treaty

The Nuclear Non-Proliferation Treaty (NPT), put into effect in 1970, is the foundation of nuclear non-proliferation today. According to the treaty, the five countries that had tested nuclear weapons by 1964—the United States, Soviet Union, England, France, and China—were permitted to keep them, with the understanding that they would eventually negotiate a way to disarm their nuclear stockpiles. The UN Security Council refers to these nations as the Permanent Five, or P-5.

All other nations are considered non-nuclear weapons states. By signing the treaty, they agree that they will not develop nuclear weapons. In return, the IAEA commits to help these nations harness nuclear power for peaceful purposes.

India and Pakistan

O ne of the primary problems underlying nuclear weapon development is that once a country with an enemy conducts a nuclear test, the other country will often do the same. This was exactly what happened with Pakistan in the 1970s, after India tested its first nuclear weapon. Although the exact numbers are kept secret, it is estimated that between the two countries, they have managed to amass 100 nuclear warheads in fewer than fifty years.

Long-Standing Tensions

For many years, India suffered under British colonial rule. After a long struggle, it asserted its independence in 1947. Unfortunately, independence did not come peacefully. India's Muslim and Hindu populations effectively split away from one another, forming two countries: India and Pakistan.

An Indian soldier stands before a nuclear-capable surface-to-surface Prithvi missile in January 2004.

As a result of this partition, large portions of India's population relocated. India remained home to the majority of the region's Hindus, and the region's Muslims settled in Pakistan. Conflict and violence grew out of these mass migrations, as well as the disputes over the location of the new border. By the time a cease-fire was called between the two countries in 1949, about half a million people had been killed.

One of the most hotly disputed territories was largely Muslim Kashmir, which became part of India. The two nations have clashed repeatedly over the right to rule Kashmir.

The periodic conflict between India and Pakistan is further complicated by their refusal to sign the NPT. Both nations have successfully tested nuclear weapons. India launched its weapons program in the 1960s. By 1974, it had managed to acquire nuclear weapon technology and tested its first nuclear weapon.

This greatly shifted the balance of power within the region. Pakistan had to consider the possible consequences that might come from confronting India, which was now a nuclear power. This power balance shifted again in April 1998, when both India and Pakistan conducted tests of their nuclear weapons. With a history of fifty years of conflict, it seemed that a war between India and Pakistan could now reach a new, deadly level. It was now possible that, if the two countries fought again, the conflict could escalate into an all out nuclear war.

India's Nuclear Program

After India broke away from England, Prime Minister Jawaharlal Nehru (1889–1964) stepped forward to lead the newly independent country. India immediately began constructing nuclear facilities. Nehru's ambitious plan was not only to acquire nuclear power but also to be self-sufficient. Although it was extremely expensive for the country, India began mining uranium and even acquired the technology to reprocess the spent fuel from its nuclear reactors. By working hard and sparing no expense, India became a self-contained nuclear nation.

In 1954, Prime Minister Nehru pushed for UN member states to adopt the Comprehensive Test Ban Treaty. Nehru initially pushed for disarmament, but his death in

1964, and China's nuclear test in the very same year, would change India's stance on nuclear weapons.

Smiling Buddha

The border of Pakistan was not the only disputed territory in India. China believed that two Indian-claimed territories along the countries' shared border rightfully belonged to China. After talks and diplomacy failed, China attacked India in October 1962, taking the territories by force. Relations between the two countries remained tense. Two years after India and China's skirmish, China tested its nuclear bomb. A brief war between India and Pakistan over Kashmir occurred in 1965, during which China supported Pakistan.

Now that China had the bomb, India felt that it needed it, too. It was possible that India would clash with China again. India had a virtually self-sufficient nuclear program, so the means to make a nuclear bomb were already at its disposal. When the NPT was drafted in 1967, India chose not to sign it.

Another factor influencing India's decision to conduct a nuclear test was its third war with Pakistan, occurring in 1971. The United States sent a naval fleet into the Bay of Bengal in support of Pakistan and as a way to show support for China, a U.S. ally. Three years later, India tested its bomb. Named Smiling Buddha, the bomb was roughly the same size as the bomb the United States dropped on Hiroshima. India had declared to the world that it was a nuclear power.

Pakistan's Nuclear Program

No one was surprised when, soon after India's nuclear test, Pakistan began trying to create a nuclear weapon. As early as 1976, Pakistan had set up a nuclear laboratory. Pakistan was unable to prove that its nuclear program was, in fact, peaceful. As a result, the United States stopped providing Pakistan with military and economic aid. This did not persuade Pakistan to abandon its program. In 1980, it announced that it had become a nuclear nation.

The Father of Pakistan's Nuclear Program

The most important force behind Pakistan's development of a nuclear program was a man named Abdul Qadeer Khan. Khan was born in India, but he moved to Pakistan in 1952, when he was still a teenager. As an adult, Khan went to work for a research laboratory in Amsterdam. During this time, he stole a number of classified documents from the laboratory. This top-secret information could be used to enrich uranium for use in nuclear reactors—or nuclear weapons.

Khan returned to Pakistan in 1976, not long after India had tested its Smiling Buddha bomb. He was picked by

Pakistan's prime minister, Zulfikar Ali Bhutto (1928-1979), to head the country's start-up nuclear program. Khan began acquiring the necessary materials to make Pakistan a nuclear power.

The Invasion of Afghanistan

Any plans the United States might have had to coerce Pakistan to abandon this course of action were interrupted in 1979. That year, Soviet troops invaded Afghanistan. At the time, the United States was concerned that the Soviet Union would not stop with invading Afghanistan, but would spread troops throughout the Persian Gulf region. Because of Pakistan's proximity to Afghanistan, the United States couldn't afford to alienate its ally. Fearing what would happen if it engaged the Soviets in direct combat, the United States instead relied on Afghan fighters, known as the

Pakistan's top nuclear scientist, Abdul Qadeer Khan, introduces the Pakistani press and public to the new Ghauri-II surface-to-surface nuclear-capable missile.

mujahideen, to do so. U.S. president Jimmy Carter, and later, President Ronald Reagan, provided funding and training for the mujahideen.

In 1982, the United States resumed giving money and military aid to Pakistan, despite qualms about that country's nuclear intentions. Concerns about Pakistan's nuclear program were set aside for the remainder of the conflict, which lasted until the final Soviet troops withdrew from the region in 1989.

The 1998 Tests

The nuclear explosions India conducted on May 11, 1998, took the world by surprise. The United States had been aware that Pakistan was actively pursuing nuclear weapons since 1983, and Pakistan claimed to be capable of uranium enrichment in 1984. It seemed likely that it would respond in kind to India's show of force.

Still, many hoped that Pakistan would choose not to respond to India's test. Bill Clinton, president of the United States at that time, had personally spoken with Pakistani prime minister Mian Muhammad Nawaz Sharif (1949–), urging him to refrain from conducting a nuclear test. Nevertheless, on May 28, 1998, Pakistan exploded five nuclear weapons in an underground test site, announcing to the world that it was a nuclear weapons state.

Managing Conflict

Conflict between India and Pakistan exists to this day. They still clash over disputed territories, especially Kashmir. Despite current Pakistani president Pervez Musharraf's (1943–) efforts to stamp out terrorism in his country, attacks by Islamic militants continue. Besides ensuring that tensions run high between the two countries, provoking armed military response that could, conceivably, spiral dangerously out of control, terrorist activity in the region presents another problem— what happens if a terrorist or radical group acquires nuclear material?

A 2006 agreement with the United States may shed some light on India's nuclear program. According to the terms of the agreement, India will allow the United States greater access to its nuclear program, and the United States will provide India with information regarding peaceful nuclear power. Until India and Pakistan decide to sign the NPT, this agreement may prove to be invaluable in preventing further nuclear tests.

4 Iraq

raq's former leader, Saddam Hussein (1937–2006), came to power in 1979. After destroying his enemies in a violent purge, he assumed leadership of Iraq's socialist Ba'ath Party. The Ba'ath Party had controlled Iraq since 1968.

Hussein was a brutal, authoritarian leader, and he ruled Iraq with an iron fist. During his rule, he had an often-turbulent relationship with the United States. In the 1990s, Iraq had fought with United States-led UN forces in a conflict known as Operation Desert Storm. In 2003, a U.S.-led coalition once again entered the country, forcibly deposing the leader. Hussein was eventually executed on December 30, 2006.

The Iran-Iraq War and WMDs

For years, conflict had existed between Iran and Iraq over their shared border. In 1980, the two nations went to war. Although the United States had misgivings about lending support to Iraq, it did not want Iran, a nation that had previously held U.S. hostages captive, to win the conflict. In 1982, the United States helped finance Iraq's war effort. The Iran-Iraq War lasted eight years, finally ending in 1988. About one million people were killed in the war, and at the end, there was no clear victor.

The Iran-Iraq War also marked the first time in decades that chemical weapons were used in combat. Today, these kinds of weapons are classified as weapons of mass destruction, and their use is illegal under international law. Tens of thousands of Iran's soldiers and civilians were killed by Iraqi chemical weapons during the war.

The Beginning of Iraq's Nuclear Program

Before becoming the ruler of Iraq, Hussein headed the Iraq Atomic Energy Commission (IAEC). It was during this time, the early 1970s, that Hussein began aggressively pursuing nuclear technology. However, in 1981, an Israeli military strike destroyed an Iraqi nuclear reactor. After that, Iraq obscured its nuclear program behind a veil of secrecy. Iraq began clandestinely purchasing uranium to use to build nuclear weapons.

By the late 1980s, Iraq was well on its way to being able to enrich uranium, which is necessary for creating a weapon. The uranium Iraq purchased often went unreported to the IAEA. However, Iraq's newly formed

Former Iraqi president and dictator Saddam Hussein salutes a crowd during a military parade in November 2000 in Baghdad, the capital city. Hussein was hanged in late 2006 by the new Iraqi government that took power following his ouster by U.S.-led coalition forces.

nuclear weapons program—which was officially begun in 1987—would prove to be short-lived. Designs for technology that would increase Iraq's capability to enrich uranium were acquired from German technicians. But Iraq's involvement in another war would put its nuclear ambitions on hold.

Desert Storm

War is expensive, and the war between Iran and Iraq cost both nations a great deal of money. Iraq was deeply in debt to a number of different countries, and its economy had been severely disrupted by the war. One of the countries that Iraq owed a lot of money to was its oil-rich neighbor Kuwait. On August 2, 1990, Iraqi troops invaded Kuwait. The UN promptly responded to this invasion by assembling a force to counter the Iraqi aggression and placing economic sanctions on Iraq. The UN force, consisting largely of U.S. troops, went to war against Iraq. During the conflict, many of Iraq's nuclear facilities were damaged or destroyed.

Iraq's military was no match for the UN troops. After an extensive bombing campaign (known as Operation Desert Storm), a ground war lasting for about 100 hours took place from February 24, 1991, to February 27, 1991. Iraq surrendered and faced the daunting task of rebuilding its ruined infrastructure. Many scientists and engineers who would have otherwise been employed in Iraq's nuclear program concentrated their energies on getting the country back on its feet. For the time being, Iraq had bigger concerns than building nuclear weapons.

Keeping Secrets

Iraq had signed the NPT, and as a result had agreed to develop its nuclear program under the IAEA's watch. During this time, Iraq began a campaign of hiding its nuclear program from IAEA inspectors, even going as far as destroying laboratories and technical equipment. Still, the IAEA managed to discover large parts of Iraq's program to enrich uranium. In July 1991, bowing to IAEA pressure, Iraq destroyed a lot of equipment used to enrich

UN inspectors prepare to leave a site in Baghdad, Iraq, after searching for weapons of mass destruction.

uranium. Further IAEA investigation uncovered a complex devoted to the research and development of nuclear weapons. Under IAEA supervision, the complex was destroyed. All other aspects of Iraq's remaining nuclear program were also confiscated or destroyed.

After the War

By 1995, Iraq had begun to comply once again with IAEA investigators, and in 1996, it gave the organization a statement completely disclosing the extent of its weapons program. By the late 1990s, the IAEA had removed all known uranium and plutonium and destroyed all known complexes that could produce nuclear weapons. It was clear that Iraq's ability to produce nuclear weapons had been effectively crippled.

Still, Hussein was prepared to pursue weapon technology if Iran once again proved to be a threat. Iraq's history of not just developing, but also using, WMDs made the international community nervous.

Additionally, the United Nations, under the urging of the United States, had imposed harsh sanctions on Iraq after its invasion of Kuwait. This meant that UN member nations were not allowed to trade with Iraq. Food, medicine, and certain medical supplies were allowed to enter Iraq. Materials that could somehow be used to produce chemical, biological, and nuclear weapons were not allowed in. For instance, Iraq was prohibited from attempting to acquire not only uranium, but also chlorine—frequently used to purify water—because it could be used to produce chemical weapons.

The sanctions took a heavy toll on the Iraqi people. Iraq's economy was in ruins. The UN hoped that the effects of these sanctions would cause Saddam Hussein to change his policies of aggression toward neighboring countries. The UN also hoped that it would make the Iraqi leader fully comply with the IAEA. The UN didn't know whether Hussein was hiding WMDs in Iraq. Since the Iraqi leader had stopped allowing UN weapons inspectors into Iraq in 1998, there was no way to tell.

A Second War

Pressure from the international community began to wear on the stubborn Iraqi leader. Finally, in 2002, a UN weapons inspection team was allowed to enter Iraq. After conducting a thorough inspection of the country, it determined that Iraq's nuclear program was nonexistent. Rumors that Iraq had attempted to acquire uranium from Niger were determined by the IAEA to be false.

Still, the United States and the United Kingdom were not satisfied with Iraq's compliance with inspectors. Believing that Iraq was hiding evidence of WMDs, including perhaps chemical and biological weapons, the two countries spearheaded a coalition to invade Iraq. This controversial invasion was not sanctioned by the UN Security Council.

On March 20, 2003, troops entered Iraq. By May 1, 2003, the Iraqi army was officially defeated. Hussein was captured in December and sent to trial for war crimes. By 2007, coalition forces have uncovered approximately 500 unused chemical weapons left over from before Operation Desert Storm. The chemicals in the weapons

Iraqi women walk past an American tank in southwest Baghdad in September 2006 during the American-led occupation of Iraq. Coalition forces invaded the country based on the premise that Saddam Hussein was stockpiling weapons of mass destruction. No such weapons were ever found and may not have existed in the months before the invasion.

had badly degraded over time, however, and it was unlikely that they would have been effective.

In 2005, Iraq held its first democratic elections in decades. At the time of this writing, coalition forces are still occupying the country, engaging in armed conflict with Iraqi insurgents. No one can be sure when peace will come to Iraq. But it is clear that, for the time being at least, Iraq is no longer a nuclear threat.

5 Iran

Iran became a modern Islamic state when Shah Mohammad Reza Pahlavi (1919–1980) was overthrown in 1979 by Ayatollah Ruholla Khomeini (1900–1989), a strict Islamic leader. During this turbulent period, Iraq invaded Iran in an act of war. The long and costly war took a toll on both sides, and Iraq and Iran were economically worse off by the time a cease-fire was reached. Thousands of Iranians had been killed by Iraqi chemical weapons in the war.

Iran's Nuclear Program

Iran once had a fairly close relationship with the United States. The United States helped Iran establish its nuclear program in 1959, with the sale of a nuclear reactor. By the late 1960s, Iran had a working nuclear reactor. The country also signed the NPT. With U.S. backing, Iran was on a course to developing peaceful nuclear energy.

Having a nuclear program would firmly establish Iran as a modern industrial power. Additionally, Iran claimed to be worried about its oil reserves. Oil is an unrenewable resource, and Iran's supply would not last forever. Iran's capital city, Tehran, was already suffering from bad pollution, which would worsen with time. The responsible use of nuclear power was a possible solution to these problems.

Iran's program developed slowly until 1968, when Iran signed the NPT. Having Iran's signature on the treaty made it easier for it to cooperate with other nations on nuclear matters. The country began pouring money into its nuclear program, and the Atomic Energy Organization of Iran was established in 1974. This organization would oversee Iran's civilian nuclear activities. By 1979, when Khomeini came to power in the Islamic Revolution, Iran had become the Arab world's foremost nuclear state.

Reshuffling the Deck

Ayatollah Khomeini's ascent to power marked the end of Iran's period of peaceful international relations. Iran's relationship with the United States soured in November 1979, when Iranian hard-liners invaded the U.S. embassy in Iran and took dozens of U.S. citizens hostage. The hostages were held for more than a year before finally being released.

After the hostage crisis, not only did the United States withdraw its support of Iran, it also went on to fund Iraq's 1980 war effort against its former ally. Like many countries, Iran did not have the necessary resources to construct a self-contained nuclear program. No longer able to rely on the United States for nuclear assistance, Iran sought out other countries with which it could work.

An American hostage is paraded before the cameras by Iranian students in 1979.

By 1990, China and Pakistan became Iran's main nuclear allies, and they signed agreements to cooperate with Iran on nuclear matters. It was believed that Pakistan's A. Q. Khan helped train Iranian scientists, and in 2005, Iranian officials conceded that they had acquired technical information from Khan.

In 1995, the United States instituted sanctions against Iran. These sanctions, outlawing U.S. investment in Iran's energy industry, were renewed by George W. Bush in 2001. The United States cited Iran's poor human rights record as one reason for the sanctions and accused Iran of having active links with terrorists. The United States also claimed that Iran actively worked to disrupt peace efforts in the Middle East, specifically those involving the nation of Israel. These sanctions affected only U.S. companies; other nations were still free to trade with Iran. However, over the years, the United States would work to block Iran from making nuclear deals with other countries.

Recent Nuclear Revelations

As a member of the NPT, Iran must keep the IAEA abreast of any developments in its nuclear program. Members are not allowed to conceal any aspect of their nuclear programs, even if it does not have to do with weapon technology. Remember, the technology used to enrich uranium so it can be used as fuel can also make weapons-grade uranium. In theory, NPT member states can prove that they are not manufacturing nuclear weapons by keeping full and accurate records of their nuclear programs for the IAEA.

In 2002, it came to light that Iran had two secret nuclear sites that it had concealed from the IAEA. These sites were photographed from space by U.S. satellites. Intensive IAEA inspections of the country followed, lasting for about three years. Iran did not make it easy for the inspectors, and for good reason. By the time the investigation had ended, it had become clear that Iran had been hiding aspects of their nuclear program for twenty years.

Hidden Away

This secret program was a cause for concern. Although Iran has maintained that it is not intending to develop nuclear weapons, the IAEA uncovered evidence of highly enriched uranium at Iranian nuclear sites. This uranium was enriched far past the point necessary for use in a nuclear reactor, although it was not quite enriched enough to be used to construct a nuclear weapon. Later on, it was determined by outside investigators that Iran had actually not produced such highly enriched uranium. Instead, the presence of this uranium could be traced to "dirty" equipment that Iran had purchased from Pakistan. It took until August 2005 for this study to be completed. In the meantime, it was assumed that Iran had enriched the uranium, a very serious situation indeed.

However, Iran agreed to cooperate with the IAEA and allow more extensive inspections. At this point, the United States and the IAEA fell into a disagreement about Iran's nuclear program. The United States was sure that these discoveries meant that Iran was trying to become a nuclear weapons state. The IAEA decided that, despite having kept certain aspects of its nuclear program secret, there is no conclusive evidence that Iran was actually attempting to produce nuclear weapons. But by October 2003, it came to light that Iran had looked into developing additional equipment for uranium enrichment and had even experimented with reprocessing and separating plutonium. It is estimated that Iran is still a long way away from developing a nuclear weapon, but its continual violations of the NPT are unacceptable by IAEA standards.

Taking Action

IAEA negotiations with Iran proved to be difficult. The agency ordered Iran to stop its uranium enrichment program in October 2003. Iran consented, but then produced no evidence that it had actually ceased its uranium enrichment activities. Iran made the same promise in August 2004, but once again did not stop enriching uranium. Even with the United States requesting that the UN consider imposing sanctions on Iran—a very serious penalty—Iran did not back down from pursuing its nuclear program. Only by November 2004 did Iran agree to stop, if only temporarily. By April 2005, Iran was preparing to once again start enriching uranium.

Members of a group of Iranian exiles opposed to the current Iranian government march in Washington, D.C., to protest Iran's nuclear program.

It was clear that negotiating with Iran was not producing the results that the UN desired. However, there was still hope that Iran might play ball. Despite its reluctance to fully cooperate with the IAEA, the fact that Iran allowed IAEA inspectors fairly thorough access to many of its nuclear sites was better than nothing at all.

Some European nations attempted negotiations with Iran in May 2005. Iran agreed to stop enrichment until the talks came to a conclusion. However, an impending shift in Iran's government was about to change everything.

New Leadership

The former mayor of Tehran became the country's president in August 2005. This man, Mahmoud Ahmadinejad (1956–), would quickly prove to be a far different leader than Mohammad Khatami (1943–), whom he replaced. Khatami had been a fairly moderate leader who pushed for reforms in Iran's strict Islamic law. Ahmadinejad, on the other hand, was a religious conservative.

Considered by many to be a controversial leader, Ahmadinejad is against Iran having relations with the United States, refuses to recognize the State of Israel's right to exist, and has been a strong proponent of Iran's nuclear program. Although Israel has never declared itself to be a nuclear weapons state, it is believed that Israel does, in fact, have a nuclear arsenal. It is feared that conflict between the two states could potentially lead to nuclear war.

Ahmadinejad is pushing for Iran to have nuclear power. According to the Iranian president, no one has a right to tell Iran what to do with its nuclear program, not even the UN. Ahmadinejad is unconcerned over the possibility of UN-imposed sanctions against Iran, claiming that such sanctions would not hurt Iran. In fact, on September 15, 2005, Ahmadinejad claimed that he was prepared to help other Islamic nations acquire nuclear technology.

Ballistic Missile Technology

Iran has long maintained that it wants peaceful nuclear energy and is not intending to make nuclear weapons. The current supreme leader of Iran, Ayatollah Ali Khamenei (1939–), is himself against nuclear weapons. He has even gone so far as to issue a fatwa, or a legally binding religious declaration, against Iran's acquisition or use of them.

However, Iran's excessive secrecy about its nuclear program has raised a lot of eyebrows. Also, Iran's recent test of ballistic missiles have caused concern

Iranian president Mahmoud Ahmadinejad tours a heavy water plant in Arak, Iran.

within the international community. These missiles, which have a range of more than 1,000 miles (1,609 kilometers), could conceivably be fitted with nuclear warheads. While Iran is still years away from being able to make nuclear weapons, the fact that it has chosen to test these missiles at a time when it is under international scrutiny is significant. These ballistic missiles have a similar design to certain North Korean missiles, although

Iran denies acquiring any missile technology from North Korea.

Elusive Truth

At the time of this writing, there is no substantial proof that Iran is developing nuclear weapons. However, the country's continual noncompliance with the IAEA raises a lot of questions. On January 10, 2006, Iran even went as far as to reopen a uranium enrichment plant that had been closed—and sealed—by UN inspectors.

An offer by a number of UN member nations, including countries from the European Union, China, Russia, and the United States, to provide Iran with economic incentives in exchange for Iran's cessation of its uranium enrichment, was also rejected. The IAEA has referred Iran to the UN Security Council. In the face of all this, Iran refuses to back down from the position it has taken.

Iran has offered a possible solution to its nuclear ambitions, suggesting that France conduct uranium enrichment on its behalf. But in October 2006, Iran took steps to increase its production of enriched uranium. Until the nation squares its nuclear program with the international community, Iran may face sanctions.

6
North Korea

T he Democratic People's Republic of Korea (DPRK), usually referred to as North Korea, is one of the most secretive nations in the world. North Korea is also one of the few Communist dictatorships left in the world. Under the leadership of Kim Jong Il (1941–), North Korea has absolutely no diplomatic relations with the United States, a country that has placed it under sanctions for decades. Neither freedom of speech nor freedom of the press exists there, and North Koreans are not allowed to travel freely outside of the country. North Korea has faced massive food shortages for decades, and it is dependent on foreign aid to keep its people from starving.

After formally withdrawing from the NPT in 2003, North Korea became even more isolated. Then, on October 9, 2006, the nation announced to the world that it was a nuclear weapons state when it tested a small nuclear weapon.

It's safe to say that no other country in the world is as closed to outsiders as North Korea. The nation is selective about what outsiders are allowed to come within its borders, and visitors are not allowed free movement within the country. Its current diplomatic relationship with the UN could be described as rocky at best, having deteriorated heavily after North Korea's recent nuclear test.

Division

The Korean peninsula was not always divided into North Korea and South Korea. A land with a long and complex history, Korea came under Japanese rule in 1905. Forty years later, after the defeat of the Axis powers (which included Japan) at the end of World War II, North Korea became an independent state. However, there was some disagreement as to what system of governance it should adopt.

In particular, the United States and the Soviet Union had differing ideas for the newly independent nation. In a move that would foreshadow the two nations' rivalry during the Cold War years, they split Korea in two. With support from the Soviet Union, North Korea became a Communist country. South Korea, on the other hand, became a democracy.

South Korean soldiers guard the border with North Korea near the demilitarized zone in Hwacheon, South Korea. The zone was created in 1953 following the end of the Korean War in which Soviet Union–backed North Koreans fought against U.S.-assisted South Koreans.

The Korean War

The first leader of North Korea was a man named Kim Il Sung (1912–1994). He held the country under authoritarian rule from 1948 until his death in 1994, when his son, Kim Jong Il, took over.

It was not long after the establishment of a divided Korea that the North and South began to clash. On

June 25, 1950, Communist-backed North Korean forces invaded South Korea. With China backing North Korea, and the United States backing South Korea, the conflict that would become known as the Korean War lasted three years, ending with a cease-fire on July 27, 1953. The border between the two countries remained unchanged.

Although a cease-fire was called between the countries, the war between them has never officially ended. Today, North Korea has an exceptionally large military of more than one million people, making it one of the largest militaries of any nation on Earth. The North and the South have sporadically had diplomatic talks and meetings, but the two nations remain fundamentally at odds.

Ambitions of the North

Under Kim Il Sung, North Korea remained a country with a fairly stable government. But under the leadership of Kim Jong Il, things began to change. By the mid-1990s, North Korea was heavily dependent upon foreign aid to feed its citizens. Despite the influx of aid, however, famine still wracked the nation. Even though people were starving, North Korea's military did not suffer, nor did its weapons programs.

North Korea has always sought a reunification with South Korea, and as such has never forgiven the United

States for its role in the Korean War. The United States has watched North Korea's extensive military development with concern. It is difficult to determine the extent of North Korea's arsenal, nuclear or otherwise.

North Korean dictator Kim Jong Il salutes soldiers of his Korean People's Army during a Workers' Party anniversary parade in October 2005.

The Pakistan Connection

Still, it is believed that North Korea's nuclear program can be traced back to Pakistan. The two nations have traded weapons with one another for several decades. Their trading partnership stretches all the way back to the early 1980s, when they worked together to provide assistance to Iran during its war with Iraq.

In the mid-1990s, North Korea went on to supply Pakistan with long-range ballistic missiles. These weapons are capable of delivering an explosive payload many miles away. Pakistan then went on to base its own ballistic missiles on this North Korean design. The Pakistani government has emphatically denied that it paid for these missiles with nuclear technology, but suspicions remain.

A Veil of Secrecy

In 2002, U.S. president George W. Bush declared that North Korea had been operating a secret nuclear program. By 2003, the United States had enacted sanctions against North Korea. The year 2003 marked North Korea's withdrawal from the NPT, which it had signed in 1985. By 2004, it came out that A. Q. Khan had provided North Korea with nuclear information and technology. To date, Khan has been linked to spreading nuclear technology not only to Iran and North Korea, but to Libya as well. The Pakistani government has insisted that any dealings Khan may have had with North Korea were done independently of government knowledge and without its approval.

North Korea has denied that it was enriching uranium, but suspicions about what was going on inside the secretive nation's borders remained, especially after North Korea withdrew from the NPT. Inspectors were barred from entering the country, and the extent of North Korea's nuclear program became anyone's guess. There is currently no hard evidence regarding the location of North Korea's uranium enrichment program. However, it is believed that North Korea has enriched—or otherwise acquired—enough fissionable material to build several nuclear weapons.

Six-Party Talks

Negotiations with North Korea have proved to be ineffective in getting the state to renounce its nuclear program or rejoin the NPT. North Korea asserts that it has the right to have nuclear weapons. These negotiations, known as the Six-Party Talks, involved North Korea, South Korea, the United States, Japan, China, and Russia. Since North Korea withdrew from the NPT, there have been five rounds of talks, and there may be more in the future.

The talks concern the possible dismantling of North Korea's nuclear program and the possible establishment of peaceful nuclear power. In exchange for this, the parties involved in the talks agree to give North Korea rewards, such as humanitarian aid, or will consider ending sanctions.

However, the talks have borne little fruit. There has been much disagreement among the parties over how to proceed. Significantly, the United States wants North Korea to dismantle its whole nuclear weapons program. North Korea claims that it is in danger of being invaded by the United States and that its nuclear weapons are the only things keeping the country safe. It abandoned the Six-Party Talks in 2005.

By refusing to cooperate with the IAEA or practically any other entity regarding its nuclear program, North

Korea has placed itself in a difficult position. The UN Security Council has gone as far as to condemn North Korea's nuclear actions. The country is dependent on foreign aid to feed its citizens and cannot afford to alienate the few allies it has left. Under economic sanctions, it is the citizens of North Korea who will suffer the most.

The Future of Nuclear Proliferation

As for the future of nuclear proliferation, it is hard to say. Some nations who have acquired nuclear weapon technology, such as Libya and South Africa, have voluntarily given it up. At least one nation, Israel, is strongly believed to have upward of 100 nuclear weapons. It has not, however, declared that it has nuclear weapons, so this number has not been confirmed. Still other nations have the capability to produce nuclear weapons, but they choose not to do so. The international system of oversight run by the IAEA has worked well over the years, but no system is perfect. It is impossible to account for all of the world's uranium and plutonium. World leaders change, as do international politics.

As long as nuclear weapons exist, the chance that they will be used exists as well. No rational human being wants nuclear war, and keeping nuclear weapon technology from spreading is one way to limit the possibility of armed conflict. However, nuclear weapons will not go away. The future of nuclear weapons, whatever it may be, rests in the hands of the leaders—and the citizens—of the world.

Glossary

ayatollah A high-ranking Islamic cleric, or religious leader. The term "ayatollah" is a designation given to clerics of the Shia branch of Islam.

cancer An often deadly disease that involves the uncontrolled division of the body's cells. This uncontrolled cell division can spread throughout the body.

chemical weapons WMDs that spread destruction through the use of chemicals.

Cold War An extended period of struggle, lasting from after World War II until 1991, between the Soviet Union and the United States. Neither nation engaged the other in military combat.

intercontinental ballistic missile (ICBM) A long-range missile that can be fitted with a nuclear warhead.

nuclear weapons Weapons capable of causing a nuclear explosion.

paranoid A state of unreasonable and irrational concern for one's safety.

plutonium A metallic element. Plutonium is radioactive, and a certain variety of plutonium—plutonium-239—can be used to make nuclear weapons.

safeguard A method of restriction or protection.

sanction A kind of punishment often placed on countries that refuse to cooperate with international law.

Sanctions generally involve the withholding of a
certain kind of goods or service.

stockpile A collection of arms or weapons, such as
nuclear weapons.

Union of Soviet Socialist Republics (USSR) A Communist
nation consisting of present-day Russia and a number
of surrounding nations. The Soviet Union fell apart
in 1991.

United Nations (UN) Established in 1945, the United
Nations is an international organization dedicated
to resolving conflicts between nations. Although
countries do not have to join the UN, most do. At
the time of this writing, there are 192 UN member
nations.

uranium A radioactive metallic chemical element. Two
kinds of uranium, uranium-233 and uranium-235,
can be used as fuel in nuclear power plants or to
make nuclear weapons.

weapons of mass destruction (WMDs) Nuclear, chemical,
and biological weapons are collectively known as
weapons of mass destruction. These weapons can
kill large numbers of people.

For More Information

Carnegie Endowment for International Peace
1779 Massachusetts Avenue NW
Washington, DC 20036-2103
(202) 483–7600
Web site: http://www.carnegieendowment.org

Center for Arms Control and Non-Proliferation
322 Fourth Street NE
Washington, DC 20002
(202) 546-0795
Web site: http://www.armscontrolcenter.org

International Atomic Energy Agency
IAEA Office at the United Nations
1 United Nations Plaza
Room DC-1-1155
New York, NY 10017
(212) 963-6010
Web site: http://www.iaea.org

Union of Concerned Scientists
National Headquarters
2 Brattle Square
Cambridge, MA 02238-9105

(617) 547-5552
Web site: http://www.ucsusa.org

United Nations
UN Headquarters
First Avenue at 46th Street
New York, NY 10017
Web site: http://www.un.org

Web Sites

Due to the changing nature of Internet links, Rosen
Publishing has developed an online list of Web sites
related to the subject of this book. This site is updated
regularly. Please use this link to access the list:

http://www.rosenlinks.com/itn/nsnw

For Further Reading

Cheney, Glenn Alan. *Chernobyl: The Ongoing Story of the World's Deadliest Nuclear Disaster.* New York, NY: New Discovery, 1993.

Havrysh, Tetiana, and Maureen McQuerry. *Nuclear Legacy: Students of Two Atomic Cities.* Columbus, OH: Battelle Press, 2000.

Hersey, John. *Hiroshima.* New York, NY: Vintage Books, 1999.

Jungk, Robert. *Brighter Than a Thousand Suns: A Personal History of the Atomic Scientists.* New York, NY: Harcourt Brace, 1958.

Mayell, Mark. *Nuclear Accidents.* San Diego, CA: Lucent Books, 2003.

Streissguth, Thomas. *Nuclear Weapons: More Countries, More Threats.* Springfield, NJ: Enslow Publishers, 2000.

Stux, Erica. *Enrico Fermi: Trailblazer in Nuclear Physics.* Springfield, NJ: Enslow Publishers, 2004.

Bibliography

Albright, David. "How Much Plutonium Does North Korea Have?" *Bulletin of the Atomic Scientists*, Vol. 50, No. 5, September/October 1994, pp. 46–53. Retrieved October 2006 (http://www.thebulletin.org/article.php?art_ofn=so94albright).

BBC News. "India and Pakistan: Tense Neighbors." December 16, 2001. Retrieved October 2006 (http://news.bbc.co.uk/2/hi/south_asia/102201.stm).

Cohen, Stu. "Iraq's WMD Programs: Culling Hard Facts from Soft Myths." Central Intelligence Agency Press Releases and Statements. November 28, 2003. Retrieved October 14, 2006 (http://www.fas.org/irp/news/2003/11/cia112803.html).

Comprehensive Nuclear-Test-Ban Treaty. UN.org. Retrieved October 2006 (http://disarmament2.un.org/wmd/ctbt/index.html).

Cooper, Mary H. "Nuclear Proliferation and Terrorism." *CQ Researcher*, Vol. 14, No. 13, April 2, 2004, pp. 297–320. Retrieved October, 2006 (http://www.iaea.org/NewsCenter/Focus/cqr_proliferation.pdf).

Coughlin, Con. "Iran Has Missiles to Carry Nuclear Weapons." Telegraph.co.uk. April 7, 2006. Retrieved October 14, 2006 (http://www.telegraph.co.uk/news/

main.jhtml?xml=/news/2006/04/07/wiran07.xml& sSheet=/news/2006/04/07/ixnewstop.html).

Goldschmidt, Pierre. *The Increasing Risk of Nuclear Proliferation: Addressing the Challenge*. IAEA.org. November 26, 2003. Retrieved October 2006 (http:// www.iaea.org/NewsCenter/Statements/DDGs/2003/ goldschmidt26112003.html).

Jungk, Robert. *Brighter Than a Thousand Suns: A Personal History of the Atomic Scientists*. New York, NY: Harcourt Brace, 1958.

"The Long, Long Half–Life." *The Economist*, Vol. 379, Issue 8481, June 10, 2006. Retrieved October 2006 (http://search.ebscohost.com/login.aspx?direct=true& db=aph&AN=21142930&site=ehost-live).

Niksch, Larry A. "North Korea's Nuclear Weapons Program." CRS Report for Congress. August 1, 2006. Retrieved October 2006 (http://fpc.state.gov/ documents/organization/71870.pdf).

Powell, Bill. "When Outlaws Get the Bomb." *Time*. October 23, 2006. Retrieved October 2006 (http://www.time.com/time/magazine/article/ 0,9171,1546342,00.html?cnn=yes).

Ramana, M. V. *India's Nuclear Program—From 1946 to 1998*. International Network of Engineers and Scientists Against Proliferation. Retrieved October 2006 (http://www.inesap.org/bulletin16/ bul16art02.htm).

Squassoni, Sharon. "Iran's Nuclear Program: Recent Developments." CRS Report for Congress. September 6, 2006. Retrieved October 2006 (http://fpc.state.gov/documents/organization/72449.pdf).

Weiss, Leonard. "Atoms for Peace." *Bulletin of the Atomic Scientists*, Vol. 59, No. 6, November/December 2003, pp. 34–41, 44. Retrieved October 2006 (http://www.thebulletin.org/article.php?art_ofn=nd03weiss).

Windrem, Robert, and Tammy Kupperman. "Pakistan's Nukes Outstrip India's, Officials Say." NBC News. October 23, 2003. Retrieved October 2006 (http://www.msnbc.msn.com/id/3340687).

Index

About the Author

Steve Minneus is a writer living in upstate New York. He's had a lifelong interest in international politics.

Photo Credits

Cover (top), p. 49 © KCNA via Korean News Service/AFP/Getty Images; cover (bottom left) © Raveendran/AFP/Getty Images; cover (bottom right) © Joe Raedle/Getty Images; p. 4 © Bradbury Science Museum/Joe Raedle/Getty Images; p. 6 © Koichi Kamoshida/Getty Images; p. 9 © STF/AFP/Getty Images; pp. 12, 35 © AFP/Getty Images; p. 13 © Marc Garanger/Corbis; p. 14 Library of Congress Prints and Photographs Division; p. 15 © Samuel Kubani/AFP/Getty Images; p. 17 © Keystone/Getty Images; p. 19 © Richard Ellis/Getty Images; p. 20 © Emmanuel Dunand/AFP/Getty Images; p. 24 © Usman Khan/AFP/Getty Images; p. 27 © Marco DiLauro/Getty Images; p. 29 © Karim Sahib/AFP/Getty Images; p. 31 © Oleg Nikishin/Getty Images; p. 34 © Paul Schemm/AFP/Getty Images; p. 37 © MPI/Getty Images; p. 41 © Nicholas Kamm/AFP/Getty Images; p. 43 © Atta Kenare/AFP/Getty Images; p. 45 © Jung Yeon-Je/AFP/Getty Images; p. 47 © Kim Jae-Hwan/AFP/Getty Images.

Designer: Tom Forget; **Photo Researcher:** Amy Feinberg